spick
and span

Scrub a dub, dub!
Super duper clean.
Inky pinky clean.

scrub
scrub
spick
and span

Neat and tidy.
So tidy and so neat.

Tyrone has a place for everything,
and everything's in its place.

gleam
spick
and span

'Argh! What's this?'

Where did it come from?
How did it get here?
Who does it belong to?
What is it?

'It's a box. It's a big box!'

This box *will* have to go!

Where can it go?

The box is shuddering!
The box is muttering!
The box is stuttering!

Oh no!

Vroom Vroom...
Vrooom Vroooooom...

The box is tearing...

The box is bursting...

The box is alive!

'What *is* it?
It *looks like*...
It's... a Dust 'o' Matic Whoover!'

Vroom Vroooom...
Vrooooom!

Dust 'o' Matic Whoover

From
Auntie Ethel 'o' Saurus
XXXXX

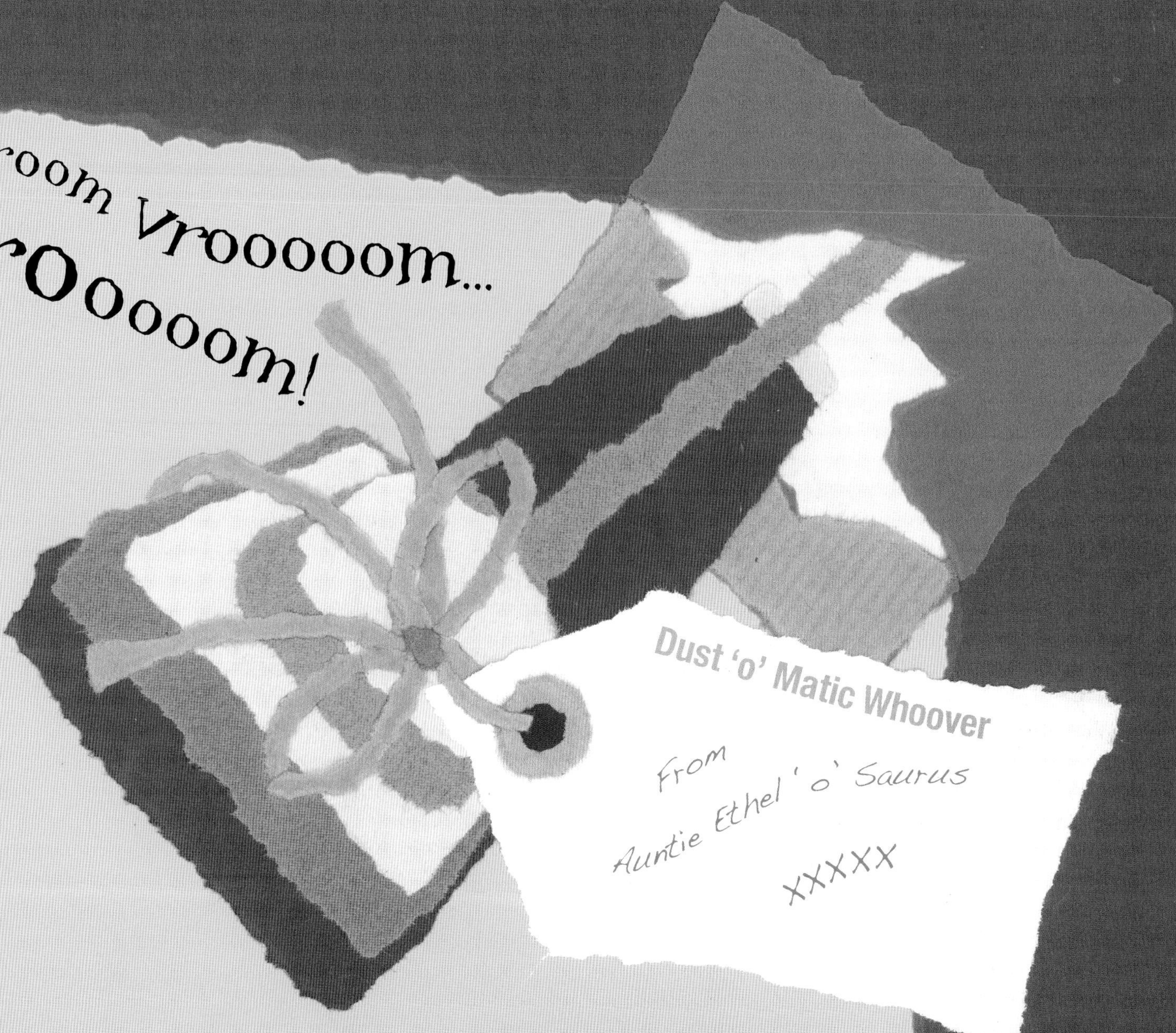

Vrrrroom Vrooooom...

Vrrrroom Vrooooom...

Vrrr room vrooooom...

Tyrone has a place for everything, and everything has a place.

'Neat and tidy. Clean and bright!'

'What **bliss**' said Tyrone. 'I know where you're going to be tonight.'

ZZZZZZZ
ZZZZZZZZZ
Gleam
sparkle

Vrooom Vroom Vroooooom...

Vrrrroom Vroooooom...

Vrrrroom Vroooooom...

Vrrrroom Vroooooom...

spick and span